AN ALLIGA
NAMED...
ALLIGATOR

by
Lois G. Grambling

Illustrations by Doug Cushman

Alligator
for Sale
FREE!

BARRON'S

New York • London • Toronto • Sydney

This is for the adult gang—
Art, Jeff, Mark, and Gail...
and for Lara and Tyler, too,
of course.

All inquiries should be addressed to:
Barron's Educational Series, Inc.
250 Wireless Boulevard
Hauppauge, NY 11788

International Standard Book No.
0-8120-6224-8 (hardcover)
0-8120-4756-7 (paperback)

Library of Congress Catalog Card No. 91-14400

Library of Congress Cataloging-in-Publication Data

Grambling, Lois G.
       An alligator named Alligator / by Lois G. Grambling ; illustrated
    by Doug Cushman.
           p.   cm.
       Summary: Elmo tries to hide his new pet alligator from his family.
       ISBN 0-8120-6224-8
       [1. Alligators—Fiction. 2. Pets—Fiction.]   I. Cushman, Doug,
    ill.   II. Title.
    PZ7.G7655A1   1991
    [E]—dc20   91-14400
                                                                         CIP
                                                                          AC

PRINTED IN HONG KONG

1234   9927   987654321

Ever since Elmo could remember
he had always wanted an alligator.

But…
every time he asked for one
his mother said, "NO!"
His father said, "NO!!"
His sister said, "YOU'RE CRAZY!!!"

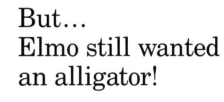

But…
Elmo still wanted
an alligator!

One day
walking home
from school
Elmo saw a sign
in someone's
front yard.

Elmo rang the doorbell....

Elmo decided not to tell his father
about Alligator.
He decided not to tell his mother
about Alligator.
He decided not to tell his sister
about Alligator.
"Someday," he said smiling,
"I'll just surprise them."

One morning, later that week, Elmo's sister went into the bathroom to wash her hair. Alligator was already there!
"Help!" screamed Elmo's sister, running out the bathroom door and down the hall. "There's an alligator in the bathroom!"

"Nonsense," said Elmo's father. "There are no alligators in this house!"

But…
Elmo knew better.
He hurried down the hall to the bathroom,
brought Alligator back to his room,
and closed the door.

One afternoon, later that week,
Elmo's mother went into the kitchen
to make herself a cup of tea.
Alligator was already there!
"Help!" screamed Elmo's mother, running
out the kitchen door and down the hall.
"There's an alligator in the kitchen!"

"Nonsense," said Elmo's father.
"There are no alligators in this house!"

But…
Elmo knew better.
He hurried down the hall to the kitchen,
brought Alligator back to his room,
and closed the door.

One evening, later that week,
Elmo's father went into the living room
to watch his favorite TV program.
Alligator was already there!
"EGADS!" yelled Elmo's father.
"There IS an alligator in this house!!"

"Oh!? Really!?" said Elmo's sister.
"Oh!? Really!?" said Elmo's mother.
"YES! REALLY!!" said Elmo's father.
"ELMO! COME HERE!! IMMEDIATELY!!!

The next day a sign appeared in
Elmo's front yard. It said,

>Alligator
>Available
>free to right person
>Inquire within

Mr. Spitz rang their doorbell.

Mr. Spitz showed his business card. It said,

Spitz & Company
Makers of Fine Alligator
Belts, Handbags & Shoes
Discount Prices

Elmo looked at Alligator.
Alligator looked at Elmo.
There were tears in Elmo's eyes.
There were tears in Alligator's eyes.
Elmo's father and mother and
sister saw the tears.

Mr. Spitz left.
Alligator didn't.
Elmo was happy!
So was Alligator!
But…

Alligator
Available
free to right person
Inquire within

Mr. Huff, their next door neighbor,
wasn't happy.
One morning,
the following week,
Mr. Huff found Alligator
doing laps in his swimming pool.
Mr. Huff didn't want an alligator
doing laps in his swimming pool.
So…

Mr. Huff called Elmo's father and mother.
Elmo's father and mother called Elmo.
Elmo called Alligator.
And Alligator came right home.
Alligator was very obedient.

And…
Mrs. Smythe, their neighbor
across the street,
wasn't happy.
One afternoon,
the following week,
Mrs. Smythe found Alligator
playing catch with her pet poodle.
Mrs. Smythe didn't want an alligator
playing catch with her pet poodle.
So…

Mrs. Smythe called Elmo's father and mother.
Elmo's father and mother called Elmo.
Elmo called Alligator.
And Alligator came right home.
Alligator was very obedient.

And…
Ms. Violet, their neighbor in back,
wasn't happy.
One evening,
the following week,
Ms. Violet found Alligator
sniffing her prize purple petunias.
Ms. Violet didn't want an alligator
sniffing her prize purple petunias.
So…

Ms. Violet called Elmo's father and mother.
Elmo's father and mother called Elmo.
Elmo called Alligator.
And Alligator came right home.
Alligator was very obedient.

The neighbors were in an UPROAR!
"That alligator must GO!" they said.
"IMMEDIATELY!"

The next day
a sign appeared
in Elmo's front yard.
It said,

Dr. Zopp rang their doorbell.

Dr. Zopp showed his
business card.
It said,

Dr. Zopp
County Zoomobile
The Zoo that travels to you.
Get to know an Animal better.
call 555-6666

Elmo looked at Dr. Zopp.
Elmo looked at Alligator.
Dr. Zopp was scratching Alligator
under the chin.
Alligator's head was resting against
Dr. Zopp's shoulder.
They looked very happy together.

Dr. Zopp smiled at Alligator.
"What a fine specimen," he said,
continuing to scratch Alligator under
the chin.
"Absolutely flawless!
What a superb addition Alligator
would make to our zoo family!"

"Of course," said Dr. Zopp,
"you'd all receive free zoo passes
for as long as Alligator
was with us."
Dr. Zopp left with Alligator.

Alligator waved goodbye to Elmo as
the Zoomobile drove down the street.
Elmo waved goodbye to Alligator as
the Zoomobile disappeared around the corner.
Elmo sighed.
Already he missed Alligator!

Elmo turned and walked slowly
back into his house.
He walked down the hall
to his room…
and went in.
His eyes opened WIDE
at what he saw!

There…
resting on his pillow…
were
TWO LOVELY WHITE EGGS!
"OH! WOW! ALLIGATOR!" he said.
"THANKS!!
THANKS A LOT!!"

Elmo decided not to tell his father
about the two eggs.
He decided not to tell his mother
about the two eggs.
He decided not to tell his sister
about the two eggs.
"Someday," he said smiling,
"I'll just surprise them!"

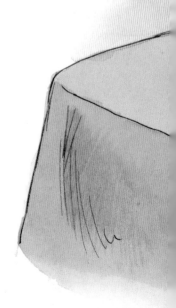

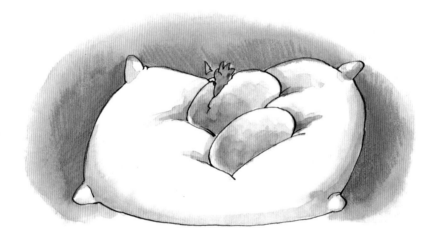